WINTER WONDERLAND

CHRISTMAS COLORING BOOK
Grayscale & Line art illustrations

includes TWO full sets
of the 23 amazing illustrations

www.alenalazareva.com

Happy coloring!

Share Your Work

Alena Lazareva's Colouring Club

A group for sharing images, inspiration, tips, techniques
and more for Alena Lazareva colouring books:
www.facebook.com/groups/alenalazareva/

Merry christmas

Second Set of Pages begins here

Share with a family member, color with a friend
Enjoy coloring your favorite images a second time
Have an extra copy in case you make a mistake

Artist

Alena Lazareva is a artist and illustrator.
Her works had been published in magazines and books of different countries (England, Australia, Italy, Russia). Her main area of focus is fantasy art, mystical beings, fairies and mermaids.

Website: www.alenalazareva.com

Alena Lazareva also has galleries and accounts at:

 facebook.com/alenalazareva.art/

 instagram.com/artlazareva/

ART PRINTS

High-quality prints, posters, cards, curtains, iPhone cases, pillows, blankets, clocks, bags are available at:
www.zazzle.com/alenalazareva
www.redbubble.com/people/alenalazareva

COLORING BOOKS
by Alena Lazareva

Grayscale Coloring books

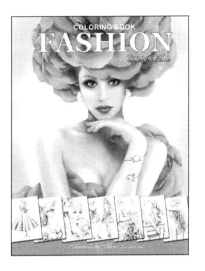

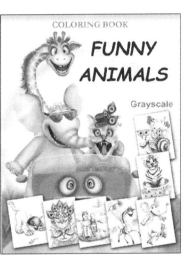

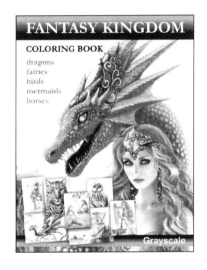

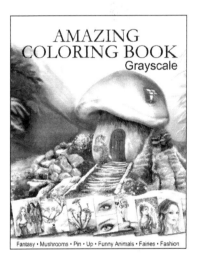

Line art Coloring books

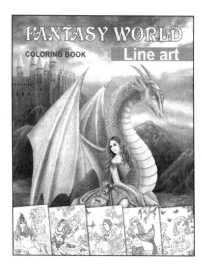

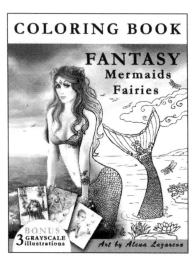

Mixed (Grayscale and Line art illustrations)

includes full color illustrations

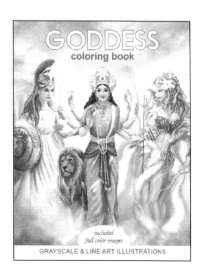

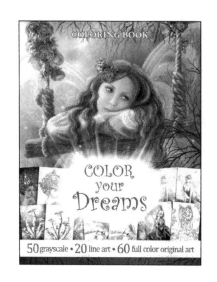

52195824R00055

Made in the USA
Middletown, DE
17 November 2017